CLICK, CLACK, Quackity-Quack

An Alphabetical Adventure

by doreen cronin
and
betsy lewin

atheneum books for young readers
NEW YORK LONDON TORONTO SYDNEY

a Animals awake

b beneath blue blankets.

Clickety-clack!

Duck dashing,

d

e eggs emptying.

f
Flippity-flip!

Goats
grooming,

g

h

hens
helping,

i

inchworms inching.

j

Jumpity-jump!

Kittens kicking,

leaping,

licking.

m

Mice munching,

n

nibbling nibbles.

Only one pig peeking.

Rain raining,

sheep sleeping.

tippity-toe

under umbrellas.

Vroom!

W

Watermelons
waiting.

marks the picnic spot.

Yawns yawning!

Z Z Z Z Z Z Z

Z Z Z Z Z Z Z Z Z Z Z Z Z.

For my bunnies

—D. C.

To Julia. Welcome to the world.

—B. L.

Atheneum Books for Young Readers
An imprint of Simon & Schuster Children's Publishing Division
1230 Avenue of the Americas, New York, New York 10020
Text copyright © 2005 by Doreen Cronin
Illustrations copyright © 2005 by Betsy Lewin
Book design by Ann Bobco
The text for this book is set in Filosofia.
The illustrations for this book are rendered in brush and watercolor.
Manufactured in China
Library of Congress Cataloging-in-Publication Data
Cronin, Doreen.
Click, clack, quackity-quack: an alphabetical adventure / Doreen Cronin ;
illustrated by Betsy Lewin. —1st ed.
p.   cm.
Summary: An assortment of animals gathers for a picnic.
ISBN-13: 978-1-4169-4101-9
ISBN-10: 1-4169-4101-0
[1. Picnicking—Fiction. 2. Animals—Fiction. 3. Alphabet.] I. Lewin, Betsy, ill.
II. Title.
PZ7.C88135Ck 2005
[E]—dc22   2004020212